Dear Parent:

Congratulations! Your child is taking the first steps on an exciting journey. The destination? Independent reading!

STEP INTO READING® will help your child get there. The program offers books at five levels that accompany children from their first attempts at reading to reading success. Each step includes fun stories, fiction and nonfiction, and colorful art. There are also Step into Reading Sticker Books, Step into Reading Math Readers, and Step into Reading Phonics Readers— a complete literacy program with something to interest every child.

Learning to Read, Step by Step!

Ready to Read **Preschool–Kindergarten**
• big type and easy words • rhyme and rhythm • picture clues
For children who know the alphabet and are eager to begin reading.

Reading with Help **Preschool–Grade 1**
• basic vocabulary • short sentences • simple stories
For children who recognize familiar words and sound out new words with help.

Reading on Your Own **Grades 1–3**
• engaging characters • easy-to-follow plots • popular topics
For children who are ready to read on their own.

Reading Paragraphs **Grades 2–3**
• challenging vocabulary • short paragraphs • exciting stories
For newly independent readers who read simple sentences with confidence.

Ready for Chapters **Grades 2–4**
• chapters • longer paragraphs • full-color art
For children who want to take the plunge into chapter books but still like colorful pictures.

STEP INTO READING® is designed to give every child a successful reading experience. The grade levels are only guides. Children can progress through the steps at their own speed, developing confidence in their reading, no matter what their grade.

Remember, a lifetime love of reading starts with a single step!

Thomas the Tank Engine & Friends

A BRITT ALLCROFT COMPANY PRODUCTION

Based on The Railway Series by the Rev W Awdry

Copyright © 2003 Gullane (Thomas) LLC
All rights reserved under International and Pan-American Copyright Conventions.
Published in the United States by Random House Children's Books, a division of Random House,
Inc., New York, and simultaneously in Canada by Random House of Canada Limited, Toronto.

www.stepintoreading.com
www.thomasthetankengine.com

Educators and librarians, for a variety of teaching tools, visit us at
www.randomhouse.com/teachers

Library of Congress Cataloging-in-Publication Data
Thomas and Percy and the dragon / illustrated by Richard Courtney. — 1st ed.   p.   cm. —
(Step into reading. A step 1 book) "Thomas the Tank Engine & Friends."
Based on The railway series by the Rev. W. Awdry.
SUMMARY: Percy is teased by the other engines when he tells them that the night before, as he
thought about the upcoming parade, he saw a giant dragon rumble by.
ISBN 0-375-82230-5 (trade) — ISBN 0-375-92230-X (lib. bdg.)
[1. Railroads—Trains—Fiction. 2. Dragons—Fiction. 3. Parades—Fiction.] I. Courtney,
Richard, ill. II. Awdry, W. Railway series. III. Thomas the tank engine and friends. IV. Series.
PZ7 .T36945935 2003 [E]—dc21   2002155038

Printed in the United States of America
First Edition 10

THOMAS and PERCY and the DRAGON

Based on *The Railway Series*
by the Rev. W. Awdry

Illustrated by Richard Courtney

Random House 🏠 New York

It is night.

Percy is sleepy.

He is thinking about
the parade tomorrow.

Percy hears a rumble.
Something is coming.
Percy opens his eyes.

He sees a dragon.
It is big and yellow
and <u>scary</u>!

"Oh no!" cries Percy.

He shuts his eyes tight.

The rumble fades.
Percy peeks.
The dragon is
running away!

The next day,
Percy rushes
into the station.

"I saw a dragon
last night!" he says.

13

"Scared little Percy!"
teases James.
"You are off your tracks!"

James chugs off.

"Peep, peep, peep!"

"You just had
a bad dream . . .

. . . dragons are not real,"
says Edward.

Percy sees Thomas.
There is something
behind him.

It is big and yellow
and <u>scary</u>!

"Watch out, Thomas!"
shouts Percy.

"There is a dragon
chasing you!"

"Silly Percy,"
laughs Thomas.
"This dragon
will not eat you.

It is a paper dragon
for the parade."

Later, Thomas and Percy
stop to watch the parade.

There is Sir Topham Hatt.

Next comes a band.

"Here comes the dragon,"
says Thomas.

"He is <u>not</u> so scary anymore," says Percy.

"You were brave to tell
me about it,"
says Thomas.

"It is good
to tell someone,"
says Percy.